WELCOME TO THE WORLD
OF
Geronimo Stilton

Published by Sweet Cherry Publishing Limited
Unit 36, Vulcan House,
Vulcan Road,
Leicester, LE5 3EF
United Kingdom

First published in the UK in 2020
2020 edition

2 4 6 8 10 9 7 5 3 1

ISBN: 978-1-78226-531-3

Text by Geronimo Stilton
Art Director: Iacopo Bruno
Graphic Designer: Andrea Cavallini / theWorldofDOT
Original cover illustration by Andrea Da Rold (drawing) Andrea Cavallini (colour)
Concept of illustration by Lorenzo Chiavini and Silvia Bigolin,
produced by Barbara Pellizzari and Christian Aliprandi
Initial and final page illustrations by Roberto Ronchi and Ennio Bufi, MAD5 (design) and Studio
Parlapà and Andrea Cavallini (colour). Map illustrations by Andrea Da Rold and Andrea Cavallini
Cover layout and typography by Margot Reverdiau
Interior layout and typography by Claire Catlin
Graphics by Merenguita Gingermouse and Gherardo di Lenna
© 2000-2015 Edizioni Piemme S.p.A., Palazzo Mondadori – Via Mondadori, 1 – 20090 Segrate
© 2020 UK edition, Sweet Cherry Publishing
International Rights © Atlantyca S.p.A. – via Leopardi 8, 20123 Milano, Italy
Translation © 2005 by Atlantyca S.p.A.

Original title: L'hai voluta la vacanza Stilton!
Based on an original idea by Elisabetta Dami

www.geronimostilton.com/uk

www.sweetcherrypublishing.com

Printed and bound in Turkey
T.IO006

Geronimo Stilton

Surf's Up, GERONIMO!

Sweet Cherry

HAVE I EVER GIVEN YOU BAD ADVICE?

Blue skies ... sandy beaches ... I was dreaming of taking a holiday. Yes, I needed to escape the rat race. I had been working **so hard** running the newspaper.

Oops, how rude. I almost forgot to introduce myself. My name is Stilton, *Geronimo Stilton*. I am the publisher of The Rodent's Gazette. It's the most popular paper on Mouse Island.

I love running the paper. But it is a lot of work. And all work and no play can make a mouse very cranky. At least that's what my great-uncle Happy Paws used to tell me. Anyway, one morning, I passed by some travel agencies on my way to the office.

The pictures in the windows looked so relaxing. *Palm trees, cheese bars by the pool …*

I sighed. Yes, it was time to take a break.

I pushed open the door to **Kick Up Your Paws**. It's one of the best-known travel agencies in New Mouse City. But before I could step inside, someone pulled my tail.

"Why hello there, **Cousinkins**!" a voice screeched in my ear. "Going on holiday?"

RATS! It was my obnoxious cousin Trap. Now I **definitely** needed to get away. That mouse can really get under my fur.

"Today must be your lucky day, **Geronimoid**," my cousin smirked. "I know exactly the agency for you." He put his paw on my shoulder. "Have I **ever** given you bad advice?"

I chewed my whiskers. One thing you should know about Trap, he's the **most untrustworthy mouse on the block!**

TRUST ME,
YOU'LL LIKE IT!

Two seconds later, my cousin whipped out his phone.

"Smoothie? Trap here. How's it squeaking?" he **SHOUTED** into the receiver. "Scrape the cheese out of your ears, my friend. I'm bringing over my cousin Geronimo Stilton. He's looking for a little holiday." He paused to pick his nose, then continued. "No, he's nothing like me, Smoothie," he chuckled. "He's not into anything exciting. No **SHARK FISHING**. No ROCK CLIMBING. He's a total scaredy-mouse. Yeah, a real *tail twirler*. You know the type. He needs a little-old-lady

10

holiday. Nothing more dangerous than some sunburned fur. Ha ha! But he's got **LOTS OF MONEY**, so don't worry about the dough. The sky's the limit with this one!"

He switched off his phone and started to scamper away.

I could not believe the nerve of my cousin. **HOW DARE HE?** I ran after him. I was fuming. "Are you nuts?" I cried. "First of all, I am **NOT** a scaredy-mouse. And second of all, I am not made of **MONEY**."

11

Trap rolled his eyes. "Well, isn't that just like you, **Germeister**," he muttered. "Such a penny-pincher. And *SO UNGRATEFUL!*"

I was about to tell him I didn't need his help when I realised he'd stopped. We had arrived. We were in a **dark alley**, far from New Mouse City's main streets. And we were standing in front of the shabbiest-looking travel agency I'd ever seen.

A sign above the window read:

Through the window, I spotted a sleazy-looking rodent. His paws rested on his desk. **I GROANED.** Something told me I *wasn't* going to like it. **No, I had a feeling I wasn't going to like it one bit!**

HELLO, GERATTIMO?

The mouse snickered when we came through the door. I wondered what was so funny. Then I stared at his outfit. Now **THERE** was something to laugh about. He was dressed in a loud Hawaiian-print shirt and shorts, even though it was the middle of **WINTER**! Dark sunglasses perched on his nose. A bracelet of green wooden beads dangled from his wrist. A tattoo on his right forepaw screamed **Aloha, Mousey**!

I was starting to feel ill. Oh, why did I think a friend of Trap's would be normal? This one looked like he belonged in a *WILD RAT ROCK BAND*!

I glanced around the room. It was packed with strange objects. They looked like souvenirs from around the world. An **ENORMOUSE** stuffed cat's head hung on one wall. I jumped. **It looked so real!**

I saw a bow and a case filled with arrows. A small card next to the arrows warned:

CAREFUL
POISONOUS ARROWS!

I jumped again. **CHEESE NIBLETS!** This place was dangerous. Other cheesy souvenirs filled the office. A large papier mâché Buddha mouse sat on the mantelpiece. A collection of yellow rubber ducks from the Quack Islands lined one wall. A tacky sequined singing sombrero with blinking red lights sat on a desk. This place was like a flea market – a flea market filled with nothing but **junk**!

Oh, why had I listened to my cousin? I should have gone to **Kick Up Your Paws**. At least their office is tastefully decorated. They even offer you a cheese snack when you walk in the door. Yes, that place was

definitely more my style: classy, sophisticated, safe!

Just then, an *EAR-PIERCING SHRIEK* filled the room. I jumped so high, I nearly hit the ceiling. Trap snickered. "See, Smoothie," he said to the sleazy-looking rodent, "I told you my cousin Geronimo is a scaredy-mouse."

It was then that I noticed the plastic cuckoo clock. A sickly-looking bird had popped out of the clock door. It shrieked out the hour, then slid back inside.

Smoothie Slickpaws took off his sunglasses and shot me a sly smile. **"Well, hello, Gerattimo!"** he shrieked, even louder than the cuckoo. "Your name is Gerattimo, right?"

I shook my head. "Ahem, well no, actually, the name is Geronimo, *Geronimo Stilton*," I corrected him.

He waved me over to a chair. "Sit down, sit down, **GERATTIMO**," he squeaked. "Don't worry about a thing. I've got your holiday all planned out. Trust me, you'll like it!"

He winked at Trap. I wondered what that was all about. But there was no time to think about it. I had to get out of this place. I didn't want some tacky mouse planning my precious holiday.

"First of all, my name is Geronimo, *Geronimo Stilton*. And I'm sorry, but I've changed my mind ..." I began.

Trap didn't let me finish. "Remember, Smoothie, only

the **BEST** will do for my cousin," he interrupted. He went on and on about how much money I had. Then he told Smoothie I needed to leave as soon as possible. "Just in case he changes his mind," Trap added, winking at his friend. "Maybe you could book him a flight for tomorrow. Or maybe even *TONIGHT*."

At this point, my head was spinning. Tomorrow? *TONIGHT?* "But what about my

luggage?" I protested. I am very big on packing. I like to be prepared. What if I forgot my fur brush? Or my underwear? Or my jumbo box of plastic bandages? Hey, you never know. I could cut my paw on a seashell or something.

Smoothie rolled his eyes. "Who needs luggage, Gerattimo?" he laughed. "All you need on one of my holidays is yourself! **Trust me, you'll like it!**"

BUT I DON'T WANT TO GO

I chewed my whiskers. What was wrong with this rodent? Were his ears filled with **CHEESE?** I opened my mouth to tell him my name was Geronimo, *Geronimo Stilton*, but it was no use. The tacky cuckoo clock had started shrieking again (I guess it was broken). And Smoothie was already typing away like a **MADMOUSE** at his computer. He spouted out names and times and dates.

"Let's see, departure at seven twenty-five from Mouse Island, arrival at ten fifty-six at San Shabby Fur Island, then there's the three-hour transfer ..."
he babbled.

I tried to stop him, but he ignored me. His eyes were glued to the computer screen. He reminded me of my nephew Slowpoke when he's playing a video game. There's no tearing that mouse away from his games.

Meanwhile, Trap began reading aloud from a brochure.

"Room with an ocean view ... complimentary organic drink upon arrival ... souvenir store ... incredible, Cousinkins. And it says here the 'personalised' transfer is included in the price!"

I was in a daze. I couldn't listen to both of them at the same time.

Plus, my ears were still ringing from that SINGING SOMBRERO.

Smoothie asked me something, and I nodded. I could not hear one squeak.

At that moment, Smoothie flicked off his computer. He turned off the singing sombrero.

Then he shook my paw. "OK, I did it!" he announced. "I've booked you a place, Gerattimo. You're flying out in two hours!"

My stomach lurched. **"WHAAAT?"** I stammered. "B-b-b-but I've decided I don't want to go."

21

Smoothie stroked his whiskers. "Sorry, **GERATTIMO**, no can do. You nodded when I asked you if you wanted to book," he explained. "Now pack your bags. It's all settled."

Trap put his paw on my shoulder. "Don't make me look bad, Cousin," he said.

"You're going on holiday, and that's all there is to it!"

He turned to Smoothie and winked. Then they danced around the office.

Hmm. Something didn't seem quite right. Why was my cousin so interested in my **holiday** plans? I just couldn't put my paw on it. Oh, well.

Two minutes later, I had my paw on something else. It was a bill for my upcoming holiday.

Smoothie snickered under his sleeve. Trap chuckled behind his whiskers.

I stared at the bill. A long string of numbers danced before my eyes. **Instantly, I fainted.**

MOVE
YOUR TAIL!

When I came to, I held up the bill. "Isn't this price a little, um, **EXPENSIVE**?" I stammered.

Trap shot me a look of pure pity, shaking his head. "Oh, **Germeister**, you are so behind the times. You really know **nothing** about the cost of things these days, do you?" he scoffed. "Tsk, tsk."

Before I could object, Smoothie jumped in.

"If you can't afford this holiday, you should have said so, Gerattimo," he added smugly. "Of course, I do offer rodents with **FINANCIAL TROUBLES** the option to pay in instalments."

My fur turned bright red. I was so **embarrassed**.

I didn't want Smoothie to think I was a cheapskate.

"Well, of course I can pay for this holiday," I muttered. I pulled out my chequebook. "And if the place really is so beautiful and classy, naturally I can understand the expense."

Trap grabbed the cheque from my paw. "Naturally, naturally," he repeated, slapping me on the shoulder. "Now, move your tail, Cousinkins, or you'll miss your plane!"

"Bon voyage!"

Smoothie shrieked. He pushed me out the door. I grabbed my tail before it got squashed like a pancake.

Thirty-five minutes later, I was at the airport. I was a nervous wreck. Did I mention I'm not into last-minute decisions? Still, I have to admit, I was a little excited.

My relaxing holiday was about to begin.

Before leaving, I called my sister, Thea. She's The Rodent Gazette's special correspondent. She would take over the newspaper while I was away. Afterwards, I called my favourite nephew, Benjamin. He is just a little mouselet, but he has the **BIGGEST heart** I know. I love him more than all the cheese in the world.

"Have a great time, Uncle Geronimo!" he squeaked. **"I can't wait to hear all about it when you get back."**

THEA

BENJAMIN

LAST GASP
AIRWAYS

At last, I climbed on board the plane. I was a little concerned. I had never flown LGA (Last Gasp Airways) before.

The first thing I noticed was the seats. They looked old and worn. The windows were streaked with dirt. And there were **dust balls** in the aisle.

I found my seat and sat down. It was hard as a rock. My tail was aching already. And what was that awful smell? I pulled a MOULDY cheese sandwich out from between the cushions. How foul.

I was wedged between an elderly lady and a young mouselet.

The elderly lady was very excited. She whispered she had never flown before.

"Don't worry," I told her. "Everything will be just fine." I'm afraid of flying, but I hoped she couldn't tell.

The young mouse on my other side made faces at me. Then he stole the cream cheese sweet the flight attendant had just offered me.

"**BRATFUR!** Give that sweet back to the gentlemouse, now!" shouted his mother.

He smirked, then took the candy out of his mouth. "Want it back?" he slobbered.

I shook my snout in disgust. He scoffed it down. Then he stuck his tongue out at me.

I felt a headache coming on. **Relax**, I told myself. *You're on holiday. Don't let a little mouselet ruin your day.*

Seconds later, **Bratfur** began pestering me with questions.

"**Why** is SAN SHABBY FUR ISLAND called San Shabby Fur? **Why** does the plane have two engines instead of four? **Why** does the toilet make

such a funny noise when I flush it? **Why** do you have fur sticking out of your nose?" he squeaked.

Meanwhile, **Bratfur**'s mother shot me a proud smile. "My little darling is always so curious. I just know he's going to do **GREAT** things someday!" she beamed.

I forced a smile. Maybe I could take a nap, I decided. But before I could even close my eyes, **Bratfur** began chattering again.

"**Why** can't I open the window? **Why** hasn't the flight attendant brought our lunch yet? **Why** are they showing that movie? **Why** do I have to keep my seat belt fastened? **Why** are you wearing those funny glasses?" he babbled.

I grabbed my headphones. Maybe I could listen to some music. Then **BRATFUR** would bother someone else. Yes, that would do the trick. I put on my favourite station, Calmmouse 101.9. Ah, the soothing music filled my ears.

Something else filled my ears, too. **RANCID RAT HAIRS! BRATFUR** was still talking to me. But now he was shrieking at the top of his lungs.

"**Why** can't I go to the toilet now? **Why** is the 'fasten your seatbelt' sign on? **Why** is the mouse over there putting his finger in his nose? **Why** are there clouds? **Why** are your ears so big?" he yelled.

By now, my head was about to **EXPLODE**. I couldn't take it anymore. I pictured myself tossing Bratfur out the emergency exit. I could just read the headline now:

STILTON MURDERS MOUSELET! PUBLISHER PUSHED OVER THE EDGE BY NON-STOP SQUEAKING!

At that moment, I heard a seat belt click.

"**Why** can't I fly the plane?" Bratfur shouted. He stormed into the pilot's cabin.

I watched in horror as he launched himself onto the control stick. **CHEESE NIBLETS!** Is this how it would all end? Killed in a plane crash by a chatterbox mouselet? I saw my life flash before my eyes.

"**Why** are you sleeping?" a squeaky voice shrieked in my ear.

My eyes flew open. **BRATFUR** was back.

"I got him just in the nick of time," the flight attendant told his mum. My head began to pound again. **Maybe crashing wouldn't have been so bad after all.**

THE FLYING TOMATO

The flight attendant began to serve lunch. I nibbled on a cracker. It tasted like cardboard.

Next I tried some blue cheese soup. It was *sour*.

I cut into the rubbery chicken. It slipped under my knife and landed in my suit pocket. Sauce dribbled down my jacket. Oh, what a **HORRIBLE** flight! First Bratfur. Now the food.

My tummy grumbled in protest. **CHEESE NIBLETS**, I was hungry! I jabbed my fork into a small tomato on my plate. It shot away like a rocket, hitting the rodent across the aisle.

He glared at me. I gulped. He was one **BIG** mouse. I'm not talking just an extra-large. He was an

EXTRA-MEGA-GIGUNDO-LARGE.

Lucky for me, right then they switched off the lights. The movie started. Everyone stared at the screen. It was a nail-biting thriller. I was glad I had already seen it. I don't like scary movies. I have to watch them with all of the lights on. Plus, I like to hug my **Cheesy** the Rat doll at the really scary parts. But don't tell my family. They'd never stop picking on me if they knew I still had **Cheesy**.

I decided to take a nap. I was **SO EXHAUSTED**.

I was half asleep when Bratfur began asking me questions about the movie. "Why is that mouse making so many **CHEDDAR CUPCAKES?**" he whined. "Is he going to a birthday party? Is he a chef?"

"No , he's not a chef," I answered, absent-mindedly. "The cupcakes are filled with poison. He's the murderer."

Bratfur let out a shriek. He jumped to his paws. **"LISTEN UP, EVERYBODY!"** he yelled at the top of his lungs. "Those are poison cupcakes. That mouse is the murderer! The cheesebrain sitting beside me just told me!"

All of the passengers gave me nasty looks. I cringed. Those poison cupcakes were starting to look pretty good.

Suddenly, the plane began to **shake**.

"All rodents kindly fasten your seat belts!" announced the captain.

The elderly lady next to me looked **worried**.

"There's nothing to worry about, madam," I assured her. "It's just a little turbulence. It will all be over soon."

She smiled and relaxed.

But ten minutes later, the plane was still rocking. I began to turn **GREEN**.

35

One minute we were up, the next we were down. Did I mention I have a weak stomach?

Meanwhile, the elderly lady next to me didn't seem to notice. She began chatting away. "I can't wait to get to SAN SHABBY FUR ISLAND. I hear they have the best octopus and garlic soup," she squeaked happily. "Then again, I think they're known for their oily sardine pizzas."

By now, my stomach was gurgling up a storm. I felt so **SICK**, I could hardly breathe. Please don't mention food again, I wanted to squeak. But the old lady kept rattling on and on. Oh, why was she so obsessed with food? Didn't they feed her down at the Creaky Mouse Nursing Home?

My stomach couldn't take it anymore. I groped for the airsickness bag in front of me.

But it was missing. Out of the corner of my eye, I saw Bratfur turning it into a paper aeroplane.

I wanted to **STRANGLE** him, but I didn't have any strength left. "Who can lend me a bag? A bag! I'm going to throw up!" I shrieked at the top of my voice.

Everyone stared at me in shock. How embarrassing. The flight attendant came running. But unfortunately, it was too late. When we reached SAN SHABBY FUR, everyone dashed off the plane. I could tell they wanted to get away from me. I did, too. **I was a stinky mess!**

SAN SHABBY
FUR ISLAND

I headed for baggage reclaim.

On the way there an **ENORMOUSE** baggage handler with bulging muscles ran over my tail with his cart ...

... a lady mouse stomped on my paw with her **high heels** ...

... Bratfur threw a glass of orange juice all over my **BEST** suit jacket ...

... I lost the keys to my suitcase ...

He He Heee!...

... I stopped in the toilets and dropped my passport into the toilet bowl.

It took me a while to fish out my passport. By then, I was ready to cry. So I sat down on the luggage carousel and began to sob like my cousin Wimpy Whiskers the time he got hit on the head with a bouncy ball. Right then, the carousel began to move. **SLIMY SWISS ROLLS!** My tail was stuck in the gears. I yanked it out.

After twenty minutes, I spotted my suitcase. Then I saw it **again** and **again**. Yes, there were seven suitcases that looked just like mine! I had to **WRESTLE** my bag away from a lady mouse who insisted it was hers.

At last, I was ready to leave the airport. I held out my passport to the customs mouse. It was stinky, just like me.

I left the airport **exhausted**. It was already late at night. I was dying to reach my hotel.

Outside it was pouring with rain. I looked around for the mouse who was supposed to meet me from the **Trust Me, You'll Like It!** travel agency.

41

WELCOME,
GERATTIMO
STILTON.
TRUST ME, YOU'LL
LIKE IT!

I spotted a slimy-looking rat carrying a sign:

WELCOME,
GERATTIMO STILTON.
TRUST ME, YOU'LL LIKE IT!

I waved him over. "Are you Gerattimo Stilton?" he asked, looking me over.

I shook my head. "Yes, I mean, no, I mean the name is Geronimo, *Geronimo Stilton*."

He stared down at his sign. "But it says here 'Gerattimo,'" he squeaked.

I took a deep breath. I practised a little meditation exercise I had learned. "Remain calm," I chanted under my breath. "Don't get upset."

"They must have got it wrong at the agency," I explained in a slow voice. "My name is **GERONIMO**. **G-E-R-O-N-I-M-O**," I repeated.

The mouse scratched his whiskers. "Are you sure?"

By now I was ready to **EXPLODE**. So much for that meditation class I took last year. Maybe I could get my money back.

"**MOULDY MOZZARELLA BALLS!** Of course I'm sure!" I screeched. "Don't you think I know my own name?"

He shrugged his shoulders. "If you say so ..." he muttered.

Meanwhile, rain had soaked through my fur. "Does it always rain so hard here?" I asked.

The rat from the **Trust Me, You'll Like It** travel agency blinked. "Didn't they tell you?" he snickered. "On the island, it either pours or it's so hot you can fry your own fur."

I put my head in my paws. **I knew I shouldn't have trusted my cousin and that slick rat Smoothie.**

What, What, What?

The next thing I knew, the rat had brought me to a car park. He pointed to a beat-up old bicycle with a funny-looking cart attached to it.

"Here you are!" he announced.

I stared at the strange contraption. "Wh-wh-what do you m-m-mean?" I stammered.

PASSENGER NO. 13
GERATTIMO STILTON
PERSONALISED TRANSFER

He pulled a piece of paper out of his pocket. It said:

Gerattimo Stilton
Personalised Transfer

"You see, this is your personalised transfer," he explained. "You need to pedal in person. The Rathole Hotel is only twenty miles away."

My head began to **POUND**. Steam shot out my ears. I am usually a very reserved rodent, but this was just too much. It was time to put my paw down.

"**WHAT?**" I shrieked so loud, I made myself jump. "Are you saying I've got to ride that bike for twenty miles? At night? Alone? In the pouring rain? Carrying my own luggage?" I was growing madder by the minute. "Well, there's no way that's going to happen, you mad mousey!" I cried. "Absolutely no possible way! No ifs, ands, or buts! No can do! Not on your life! Not for all the cheddar roll-ups in the world! I totally and completely refuse, or my name is not **GERONIMO STILTON**!"

45

TRULY A
RAT'S NEST

Ten minutes later, I was pedalling away into the night. I **really** needed to talk to my therapist about becoming more assertive.

The rain pounded down on my head. I choked back tears. My best suit was getting ruined. How would I explain this one to Starchette? Do you know her? She's the cute mouse who works down at my dry cleaners.

I started off on the main road but soon found myself on a dirt path. It led into a deep, dark forest. Rat-munching rattle snakes! Things were going from bad to **worse!**

The sky grew darker and darker. I tried to light the way with the tiny torch attached to my key. It didn't work.

I felt like my cousin Squinty before he got glasses. Everything was pitch-black.

Suddenly, the bicycle's front wheel hit a stone. The cart turned over. My suitcase flew into the air and landed on my tail. **"CHEESE NIBLETS!"** I squeaked. "I knew I shouldn't have trusted them!"

Right then, I heard the sound of faraway music. It gave me hope. Guided by the music, I pedalled for another fifteen minutes. Then I reached a clearing in the forest.

I noticed a weathered old sign. It read:

RATHOLE HOTEL

"Safe at last!" I murmured happily. But my happiness didn't last long.

I pulled up to the hotel. It was a three-storey wooden shack with a collapsed roof and broken windows. At the entrance lay a doormat full of holes. From the doorknob hung an **'ELCOME'** sign. The **'W'** was missing.

I stumbled off the bike. I was dizzy from all the exercise. Spots swam before my eyes. Still, one thing was clear to me. **The Rathole Hotel was a definite** rat hole!

ROOM 313!

I parked the bike in front of the entrance. Then I dragged my suitcase up to the door. Why, oh, why had I brought **SO MUCH STUFF**? I crawled towards the reception desk, grumbling and groaning.

There was no one in sight. I put my paw on the bell and began to ring. I rang and rang and rang furiously for at least ten minutes.

Finally, a plump mouse with thick handlebar whiskers held in place with clothes pegs sauntered out.

He was wearing a brightly striped T-shirt and loud Bermuda shorts. He yawned into my snout and mumbled, "Well?"

"Yes, I have a reservation here," I squeaked. "My name is Stilton, *Geronimo Stilton*." He scratched his tail.

"Umm, let's see ... here it says you are Gerattimo Stilton," he muttered. "Are you *sure* your name is Geronimo?"

I gnashed my teeth. My whiskers began to whirl in a rage. Why would **NO ONE** listen to me? Did they all have cheese in their ears?

"Of course I'm sure! I ought to know my own name!" I exploded. "So please take note that my name is Geronimo, **GERONIMO STILTON**! And that I'm fed up! That I'm exhausted! That I want to go to my room now! That I want to take a shower! That I want to eat something! And most of all that I want to be called **GERONIMO! GE-RO-NI-MO! G-e-R-o-n-I-m-o!**

He shot me a look of pity. "Whatever," he said with a yawn. "Guess it's a good thing you decided to take a holiday. You sure are one stressed-out rodent."

He grabbed a key and slapped it into my paw. "You're on the third floor," he told me. "And don't look for the lift. We don't have one. By the way, the restaurant is closed. But as our brochure says, **you'll find a delicious welcoming snack** on your bedside table."

ONE SMELLY CHEESE RIND

I climbed the wooden staircase, lugging my suitcase behind me.

It was then that I realised I would be staying in room **313**.

313! **HOLEY CHEESE!** Are you superstitious? I'm not really.

Well, maybe a little. OK, maybe **A LOT**. My teeth began to **CHATTER** just thinking about the number thirteen. How unlucky can you get?!

I reached my door and opened it. I switched on the light … and almost fainted.

I tried to remember the description of the room in the brochure.

... **UNIQUELY DECORATED** ...

... **SEA VIEW** ...

... **BATHTUB WITH ORGANIC HYDROMASSAGE** ...

... **OWN FRIDGE** ...

... **OWN TELEVISION** ...

I looked around. No fridge. No television. Instead, I found a dark, dingy room painted in a sickly green. The one window overlooked an open-air disco. Below, hundreds of rodents were dancing wildly to the rhythm of ear-piercing music.

I stumbled to the bathroom, clutching my nose. Did I mention the place smelled?

Instead of a bathtub there was a large, rusty metal bucket.

"This is not happening," I told myself. "This is all just a bad dream."

I sat down on the worm-eaten bed and closed

54

my eyes. "Inhale ... exhale," I chanted. Yes, I was starting to feel a teeny-tiny bit better. Two minutes later, I heard a loud CRACK. Then the bed collapsed under my weight!

I opened my eyes. That's when I spotted the plate on my bedside table. It held a piece of stale bread and one smelly cheese rind. A plastic fork with a broken tine was stuck in the rind.

The plate had been decorated with a big lettuce leaf. A snail sat in the middle of the leaf, munching away. There was an olive pit next to the leaf. I guess the snail liked olives, too.

I chewed my whiskers in frustration. Was this the 'delicious snack'? Was this the 'welcome'? Was this a JOKE? At that moment, I noticed a small greasy card by the plate. I read it to myself:

For
Gerattimo Stilton
Room 313

"**Gerattimo?!**" I squeaked, feeling the blood rush to my fur. "**Gerattimo? Gerattimo?**" I repeated, paws clenched. "**CHEESE NIBLETS!**"

I threw the window open and stuck my head out.

"MY NAME IS GERONIMO, GERONIMO STILTON!"

I screeched. The loud music from the disco stopped abruptly. A hundred rodents turned to face my window.

"Who's that madmouse?" I heard one mouse whisper.

"Must be some kinda **WACKO**," another squeaked.

"Too much sun, if you ask me," a third voice added.

Ashamed, I closed the window and drew the curtains.

What I need is a nice hot shower, I decided.

I lathered myself with soap and turned on the tap. Not a single drop of water came out! I stumbled to the phone to call the lobby. I should have known. The line was dead.

I stamped my paw in disgust and slipped on the dirty carpet. "I **knew** I shouldn't have trusted them," I groaned.

I was too tired to go downstairs to complain. I was too tired to unpack my suitcase. I was too tired to cry.

No, there was only one thing left to do. I pulled on a pair of dirty white pyjamas I found hanging in the bathroom. **Then I threw myself down on the smelly bed to try and get some sleep.**

COCKROACHES FOR BREAKFAST

The next morning I woke up exhausted, with bags under my eyes.

CHEESE NIBLETS! WHAT A NIGHT! I was kept awake by a swarm of fleas in my bed. And the noisy disco hadn't shut down until five in the morning.

I would have loved to sleep late, but I couldn't. At six o'clock, I practically flew out of my bed. A construction crew had begun **DRILLING** and **HAMMERING** right under my window. The noise was even worse than the disco music.

I headed towards the bathroom without my glasses. I was too tired to put them on.

I switched on the light, yawning.

How strange. "I could have sworn the bathroom tiles were all white, not black," I mumbled to myself.

Right then, I put my paw on one of the small black tiles. A terrible **CRUNCHING** noise followed.

My stomach lurched. Something told me this wasn't a good sign.

I ran for my glasses. Did I tell you I can't see a thing without them?

Back in the bathroom, I discovered a horrifying sight. I had squashed a cockroach!

The bathroom was full of them. **GIANT COCKROACHES EVERYWHERE!** On the floor, on the walls, and even on the ceiling.

At that very moment, a cockroach fell off the ceiling and landed inside the collar of my pyjamas. It crawled all the way down my back.

I let out a *HORRIFIED SCREAM* that woke the entire hotel.

Ten seconds later, someone banged on the wall.

"What's going on?" I heard a mouse ask.

"Who screamed?" another cried.

"It's that Stilton again, Gerattimo Stilton," someone else answered.

I cringed behind the door. How **embarrassing**. I listened to the crowd gathering in the hallway. They were all talking. Yes, talking about yours truly.

"Him again?" a rodent huffed.

"Yes, it's that **CHEESEBRAIN** who arrived yesterday," a voice grumbled.

"Ah, you mean the mouse who wants to be the centre of attention?" a rodent muttered.

"Too much sun, if you ask me," someone else muttered.

I had stopped screaming. But now I was purple with shame!

I Can't Open My Suitcase!!!

I went to look for my toothbrush. Then I remembered I had lost the key to my suitcase. I tried all the ways I could think of to open the lock. First, I inserted a paper clip. Then I tried picking it with a cheese knife. I even tried hammering the lock with the doorstop. Still, it wouldn't budge.

Getting more desperate by the minute, **I SMASHED IT** against the wall.

Nothing happened.

I was ready to smash myself against the wall. **I NEEDED MY STUFF!** I wanted to brush my teeth. I wanted to put on a clean pair of underwear.

"Rats!" I shrieked, giving the suitcase a hard kick. It went **flying** out over the balcony.

I scrambled downstairs to go get it. It **STILL** hadn't opened.

I dragged it back to my room. **Then I sat down on it and cried.**

WHAT ELSE COULD I DO?

I'm Too Sexy For My Fur!

I decided the first thing to do was buy myself a new swimsuit.

I went in search of the hotel gift store.

The store was dark and dusty. A scruffy-looking mouse sat with his paws up on the counter.

"I need swimming trunks," I told him. He pointed to a rack. There was only one pair of trunks hanging from it. They had purple and yellow stripes with tacky satin hearts. The tag inside read

I'm too sexy for my fur!

It was the most **hideous** thing I have ever seen. Plus, the trunks were three sizes too big for me.

"Do you have something less flashy, in a smaller size?" I asked the shop assistant.

He shook his head. "Nope, that's it. Take it or leave it."

I blinked. "But these don't fit me," I protested. "And besides, I don't like them."

"Well then, don't take them," he mumbled.

"But I need them!" I cried.

"WELL THEN, TAKE THEM!" he shouted in my ear.

I pulled out my wallet to pay for the swimming trunks. That's when I saw the price tag.

Pound signs swam before my eyes. "Why is this so **expensive?!**" I shrieked.

"It's one of a kind," the sales clerk smirked. "You'll make a real fashion statement."

I groaned. I'd make a real statement, all right. **I'd be the most ridiculous-looking rodent on the beach!**

65

EVERYTHING A.P.B
(AS PER BROCHURE)

I went to speak with the hotel manager. My whiskers were quivering in anger. I had a list of complaints a mile long. I mean, the brochure listed this place as a resort. But it was clearly a **DUMP**.

The manager listened to me with a **funny look** on his face. He didn't seem too surprised by my gripes. "Come with me and I'll explain everything," he said.

We went up to my room. Then he began to read from the brochure. "Let's see, you booked a room with unique decorating features," he read. He waved his paw around the room. "Have you ever seen a room painted in such a shade of **MOULDY GREEN?** Pretty unique, wouldn't you say?" He grinned. "Therefore, it is **A.P.B.** (As Per Brochure)."

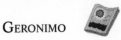

My head began to pound. "But what about the **sea view?**" I protested.

He snickered. I was getting the impression I wasn't the first rodent to complain. He pulled out a small pair of binoculars from his pocket. "Ok, if you lean out as far as you can over the balcony, turn left, stretch your neck, pop out your eyes, and use these binoculars, you'll have your sea view! Yep, that's **A.P.B.** (As Per Brochure)."

I chewed my whiskers.

"B-b-but what about the b-b-bathtub with the organic hydromassage?"

Once again he snickered. He went into the bathroom and pointed to the dented washtub.

"Here is your tub," he said. Then he pulled a whisk from his other pocket. "And here is your hydromassage!"

He put the whisk into
the water and began
turning it furiously.

"See what I mean? Yep, that's **A.P.B** (As Per
Brochure) for sure!" he chuckled.

By now, I was seething with rage. "But what about
having my **own fridge** and my **own television?**"

"Well, that's pretty obvious!" the manager chuckled.
"It means you should have brought your own!
Yessiree, that one is definitely **A.P.B.** (As Per
Brochure)!"

Finally, I couldn't take it anymore. I was so mad, I
had twisted my tail up like a pretzel.

"BROCHURE?!" I exploded. "I don't give a whisker about the brochure! This place is **RIDICULOUS!** This place is **PREPOSTEROUS!** This place isn't fit for a flea!"

Just then, someone from next door banged on the wall. I could hear the comments flying:

"Who's the **MADMOUSE** shouting at the top of his lungs?" someone cried.

"It's that Stilton again, Gerattimo Stilton," another squeaked.

"He's really lost his marbles now!" a third rodent added.

"Too much sun, if you ask me," someone else muttered.

How embarrassing.

A RUBBERY CROISSANT

I decided a nice breakfast would cheer me up. There was a long line of mice leading into the dining room.

"Did you get your number?" a mouse with a terribly burned snout asked me.

"Number? What number?" I asked.

Snout Burn pointed to the line. "The number for your place in line. It takes at least three hours to get breakfast around here," he said.

I sighed. **I KNEW I SHOULDN'T HAVE TRUSTED THEM!**

I took my place in line. My stomach was grumbling like my uncle Cheesebelly when they run out of cheese rolls at the bakery. I hadn't eaten anything since that awful cheese rind the night before. I was **STARVING.**

Just then, I noticed a mouse carrying a tray of croissants, tea, and coffee for sale. I couldn't resist. I was so hungry. I bought a small croissant and a cup of coffee. The croissant tasted like **RUBBER**. The coffee tasted like **MUD**.

"That'll be thirty pounds, please," squeaked the mouse.

"What?" I squeaked. "That's highway robbery!"

The mouse just snickered. "Take it or leave it."

What could I do? I paid him the money.

Rats! I knew I shouldn't have trusted them!

How Much Farther to the Beach???

After breakfast, I headed for the beach. I followed the long path through the sand dunes. I walked and walked and walked. An hour later, I was **STILL WALKING**. Did I mention the path was long? The sun scorched my fur. I was dying of thirst. I mean, really DYING.

Suddenly, I had a horrifying thought. What if I really did die of thirst? Headlines flashed before my eyes:

STILTON SIZZLES TO A CRISP! PARCHED PUBLISHER: ALL DRIED UP AND NO PLACE TO GO!

Just then, I spotted something up ahead. It was a lemonade stand. "How much farther to the beach?" I asked the vendor.

He smirked. "Just another hour," he said. I felt faint. Another hour? I would **NEVER MAKE IT!**

I gulped down a glass of lemonade.

"That'll be fifty smackeroos. Cash only," the mouse said, grinning evilly.

I pulled out my wallet. What else could I do?

I knew I shouldn't have trusted them!

A Scooter Worth Its Weight in Gold

I kept on walking under the burning sun. After a little while, I saw another vendor. This one was renting out scooters.

"Ahem, how much for a scooter?" I asked cautiously.

"Don't worry, we take credit cards," the mouse replied.

I immediately started to worry.

This little holiday was costing me a **fortune!** I was going to have to eat only mac and cheese when I got back home. Yep, no more fancy dinners for me after this trip. I was going **BROKE**!

Just as I thought, the scooter was worth its weight in gold. At last, I reached the beach. I looked like a **TRAIN WRECK**. My tongue was hanging out of my mouth from the heat. My snout was sunburned. And my left paw was longer than my right paw. Oh, but that's another story.

I was welcomed by a lifeguard as big as a house. He was wearing an itty-bitty yellow swimsuit and an extra-tight tank top that read 'Rathole Hotel Beach.' On his bulging right bicep, he had a tattoo of a beautiful female mouse. He had a thick gold chain around his neck, and his hair gleamed in the sun. What an **ATHLETE!** What a **MUSCLE MOUSE!** What a **SHOW-OFF!**

He held out his paw. "Call me **CRUSHER**," he said, squeezing my paw in his. I yelped. When he released me, I checked for broken bones.

CRUSHER didn't seem to notice my pain. He pulled out a pad with a list of names on it. "You must be Gerattimo Stilton," he said. "I've been expecting you."

"Geronimo, not Gerattimo," I corrected him wearily.

He stared at the pad again. "Are you **sure** your name is Geronimo?" he mumbled. "It says Gerattimo here."

I was so tired I could barely squeak. "My name is Geronimo, *Geronimo Stilton*," I whispered.

He scratched his tail. "If you say so ..." he muttered.

I could tell he didn't believe me.

SUCH A PLAYFUL MOUSE ...

CRUSHER led me to my beach umbrella. The tag said:

313 – *Gerattimo Stilton*

I pretended not to see it so I wouldn't have to complain. Instead, I looked around. The beach was mobbed. The rat sitting on my left had his radio cranked up to an ear-splitting volume. On my right sat **Bratfur**. Yes, it was that obnoxious young mouselet who had been sitting next to me on the plane. **RATS!** I had the **WORST LUCK**!

As he was leaving, **CRUSHER** pointed to the water. Then he shouted something, but I couldn't hear him. The music was so loud. **"WHAT DID YOU SAY?"** I shouted. But he was already gone.

Two minutes later, I got hit with a bucketful of **ICE-COLD WATER.**

I whipped around. Then I sighed. It was **BRATFUR**, of course.

His mother smiled. "He's such a nice playful mouse, don't you think?" she laughed.

I shut my snout. I was following my aunt Sweetfur's advice. She always told me, **"If you don't have anything nice to squeak, don't squeak anything at all."**

As Pale as a Piece of Mozzarella

It didn't take **Bratfur** long to begin pestering me with his questions. "**Why** is the sun hot? **Why** is the water wet? **Why** does the sand burn your paws? **Why** does the lifeguard have all those muscles? **Why** don't you have any muscles?" he chattered.

I pretended to be **ASLEEP**. It didn't stop him. "**Why** do I have to put on sun cream? **Why** was it raining yesterday and today it's sunny? **Why** do fish like water? **Why** do seagulls have white poo? **Why** are you as pale as a piece of mozzarella?" he babbled.

Meanwhile, the rat on my left was tapping his paw to the rhythm of the music. He was kicking up clouds of sand.

"Er, excuse me, could you stop covering me in sand?" I asked him politely.

"What band? There's no band here!" he replied.

I shook my head. "No, the **sand!**" I repeated a little louder this time.

He looked confused. "What? Land? No, planes don't land here!" he yelled.

I chewed my whiskers. "Not land. I said **'sand'!**" I shrieked.

The rat just shrugged his shoulders. He closed his eyes and started tapping his paw even faster to the beat of the music.

Finally, I couldn't take it anymore. I switched off his radio and shouted at the top of my lungs, "Sand! SAAND! You're covering me in **saaaaaaaaand!**"

"It's him again, isn't it?" I heard one bather comment.

"Yes, it's that Gerattimo Stilton!" another replied.

"What is his problem?" someone else asked.

"He should be ashamed of himself!" a rodent added.

"Too much sun, if you ask me …" another mumbled.

Purple with shame, I tried to hide behind my newspaper.

After a while, I realised I was getting **SUNBURNED**. I decided to buy some sun cream. Right at that moment, I saw a vendor passing by. He pulled out a tiny tube of sun cream. "You'll need one with a 90 SPF. You're as pale as a piece of mozzarella!" he said knowingly.

"That'll be one hundred buckaroos, please."

My eyes nearly popped out of my head. "What a **rip-off!**" I squeaked. Then I paid him. Forget the cheese! **I would only be able to afford macaroni after this holiday!**

SWIMMING WITH SHARKS

I decided to go for a swim. I noticed there wasn't a single mouse in the water. *Perfect!*

I put on my flippers, my swimming hat and my earplugs, and plunged in. I floated lazily out to the open sea. After a while, I noticed that a small boat was following me. The lifeguard on board waved his paws at me. It was **CRUSHER**. I guess he thought I might be afraid of the deep water. I waved back and smiled to let him know I was OK.

But **CRUSHER** kept following me. Then he started yelling something. I took out my earplugs as the boat came closer.

"**Look out for sharks!**" I heard **CRUSHER**

shriek. At the same time, I heard something else. A loud splashing sound right behind me. **CHEESE NIBLETS!** Out of the corner of my eye, I noticed a gleaming fin. A shark was right on my tail!

Ten seconds later, a paw reached out and grabbed me. It was **CRUSHER**. He pulled me onto his boat. Then he motored back to shore. "I told you to watch out for the sharks, Geronimo," **CRUSHER** scolded me.

When I got out of the boat, everyone was staring at me.

The comments were flying.

"It's that Gerattimo Stilton **again**!" one rodent huffed.

"Swimming with the **SHARKS** just to get himself noticed!" another griped.

"What a **CHEESEHEAD**!" someone else snorted.

"Too much sun, if you ask me … " another mouse mumbled.

How **EMBARRASSING!** Quiet as a mouse, I ducked under the umbrellas. **Then I scampered away.**

5:30 A.M.
BUNGEE JUMPING

It had been a **DISASTROUS** day.

I fell into bed, exhausted, that night. Tomorrow I'm going to sleep until noon, I decided. I'm supposed to be on holiday, right? Or maybe I'd just stay in bed the whole day.

I fell into a restless sleep. The disco music **ROARED** in my ears.

At five o'clock in the morning, I was woken up by a knock at my door.

"Who is it?" I mumbled.

"WAKE UP, GERATTIMO! TIME TO LEAVE!"

squeaked a voice on the other side of the door.

I opened it. It was another **MUSCLE MOUSE**. This one was even bigger than **CRUSHER**. He looked like he lifted weights in his sleep.

"Did you forget, Gerattimo?" he cried. "You're booked for a bungee-jumping lesson this morning."

I didn't understand. "**WHAT?** But I didn't ..." I stammered.

Before I could go on, Muscle Mouse stuck a piece of paper under my snout.

87

IT READ:

5:30 a.m. BUNGEE JUMPING
GERATTIMO STILTON

7:30 a.m. HANG-GLIDING
GERATTIMO STILTON

11:30 a.m. DEEP-SEA DIVING
GERATTIMO STILTON

12:30 p.m. ARCHERY
GERATTIMO STILTON

2:00 p.m. FREE-FALL PARACHUTING
GERATTIMO STILTON

7:00 p.m. ROCK CLIMBING
GERATTIMO STILTON

5:30 a.m. BUNGEE JUMPING
– GERATTIMO STILTON

7:30 a.m. HANG-GLIDING
– GERATTIMO STILTON

11:30 a.m. DEEP-SEA DIVING
– GERATTIMO STILTON

7:00 p.m. ROCK CLIMBING
– GERATTIMO STILTON

2:00 p.m. FREE-FALL PARACHUTING
– GERATTIMO STILTON

Muscle Mouse gave me a friendly slap on the back. It sent me flying across the room. I crashed into the dresser. I wondered if I was totally paralysed or if I would be able to walk with a cane.

Muscle Mouse didn't seem to notice my pain. "Are you telling me you've forgotten, Gerattimo?" he grinned.

I didn't know what to say. Of course, I hadn't signed up for such ridiculously dangerous activities. After all, I'm **AFRAID** of heights. I'm **AFRAID** of sharks. I'm **AFRAID** of pairing the wrong shirt with the wrong tie.

"Ahem, first of all, my name is Geronimo, *Geronimo Stilton* ..." I corrected him.

He smirked, waving the piece of paper under my nose.

"What a j⊙ker!" he chuckled. "It says here, 'Gerattimo.' And, Gerattimo, we've already wasted too much time. Now, get dressed and let's get going!"

I tried to protest, but he kept waving the paper under my snout. But there was no way I was going.

No way in a **million, trillion, gazillion years!**

Two minutes later, I followed Muscle Mouse down the hall. I had fallen for the old 'shake my paw' trick. When I stuck out my paw to shake, Muscle Mouse had grabbed me.

CHEESE NIBLETS, it was going to be one long day!

WHISKERS
QUIVERING ...

What can I say? The whole day was an absolute nightmare.

I **JUMPED** (or was I pushed?) off a bridge with an elastic band attached to my ankle ...

Then I **JUMPED** (or was I pushed?) off a cliff with a hang-glider strapped around me ...

Next, I **plunged** (or was I pushed?) into the sea with a heavy tank on my back ...

Yes, I think it would be safe to say it was the worst day of my life. After the deep-sea diving, I went parachuting. I was so scared, I fainted on the way down. Then I swam with the sharks. I swam away so fast, I didn't stop until I hit my beach umbrella. Finally, I went rock climbing up Mount Deadrat. Frankly, I'm amazed I'm still ALIVE AND SQUEAKING!

I headed back to the hotel with a pounding headache. What a frightening day. My whiskers were quivering with stress.

I dragged myself past the reception desk. That's when I noticed **Bratfur**.

He was busy scribbling something on the extreme sports activity board.

I snuck up behind him. **ROTTEN RATS' TEETH!** He was writing my name down after every activity.

Enough was enough, I decided. It was time to give Bratfur a **PIECE OF MY MIND**. But before I could squeak a word, his mother arrived. She gently took the pen from her son's paw. Then she stroked his ears. "My little darling is such a 𝓼𝓲𝓵𝓵𝔂 𝓳𝓸𝓴𝓮𝓻," she murmured, leading him away. Bratfur stuck his tongue out at me.

SILLY JOKER?! I wanted to scream. But I didn't. Instead, I thought about some 'silly jokes' I could play on Bratfur. Like maybe I could put itching powder on his beach towel. Or I could stick chewing gum on his pillow. Or, even better, I could lock him in his suitcase and ship him off to Tomcat Island. I was just thinking about it. Yes, a few days with some tough cats would be **just perfect for the 'little darling!'**

SEA LION-SWEAT SMOOTHIE

It was dinner time. I got in the long line. Just then, a polished-looking female mouse strolled up to me. She offered me a glass of some **STRANGE-LOOKING** liquid.

"Hello, I'm Perky, your health and relaxation director," she announced. "You look like you could really use our services." Perky chattered on about mud baths, steam saunas, and meditation classes. I was only half listening. Instead, I was staring at the drink in my paw. It had the most **DISGUSTING** smell.

"What is this?" I asked, feeling ill. **"A sea lion-sweat smoothie,"** she answered. "It's loaded with vitamins and minerals."

I tried not to gag. As soon as Perky left, I started to empty the drink into a flowerpot.

Suddenly, she reappeared at my side. "You need to drink that," she squeaked. "It's good for you!"

I blinked. "Um, thank you, it's just that ..."

"I said, drink it up. **NOW!**" she hissed. I'd had enough. I put my paws on my hips.

"I'M NOT GOING TO DRINK IT! IT STINKS!"

I shrieked at the top of my lungs.

The room fell silent.

Everyone turned around.

"Who's yelling his head off?" I heard a mouse ask.

"Must be that Gerattimo Stilton again," another answered.

"Too much sun, if you ask me," mumbled another rodent.

There Must Be Some Mistake!

That night, I fell into bed. "Tomorrow I will **DEFINITELY** sleep in", I told myself.

But at six o'clock the next morning, someone was knocking at my door. "Who is it now?" I asked, exasperated.

"It's the hotel manager, Gerattimo!" a voice squeaked. "Have you forgotten you are leaving today? You're **very late**! You're going to miss your plane!"

I opened the door in a daze. "What do you mean I'm leaving? I've paid for a whole week," I muttered.

The hotel manager just shook his head. He showed me a piece of paper from the **Trust Me, You'll Like It!** Travel agency. It read:

GERATTIMO STILTON: BOOKING FOR TWO NIGHTS

I was speechless. The hotel manager put his paw on my shoulder. "I know you want to stay longer, Gerattimo. **The Rathole** is such a wonderful hotel," he murmured. "But you must go home now. Better shake a paw. Remember, it's twenty miles to the airport. And if you don't leave now, the next available plane doesn't leave for another month."

That did it. There was **no way** I was spending another month on SAN SHABBY FUR ISLAND. I grabbed my suitcase. Then I jumped on the strange bicycle and took off like a **MADMOUSE**.

It was a very, very, very long ride. Still, I managed to catch my plane just before it took off.

I collapsed into my seat and fell into a deep, deep sleep.

The next thing I knew, a flight attendant was shouting in my ear. "Wake up, we've reached our destination, Mr. Gerattimo!"

Ah, sweet, sweet Mouse Island. I had never been so glad to be home. I smiled at the flight attendant. "The name's Geronimo, *Geronimo Stilton* ..." I said with a yawn.

Outside the airport, I hailed a taxi. "Take me to the **Trust Me, You'll Like It!** travel agency, please," I told the driver.

The taxi stopped in front of the agency. I leaped out. But I didn't get far. A card was stuck in the store window.

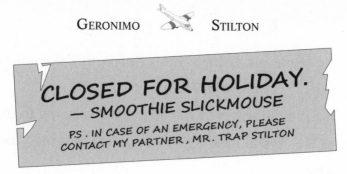
CLOSED FOR HOLIDAY.
— SMOOTHIE SLICKMOUSE
P.S . IN CASE OF AN EMERGENCY, PLEASE
CONTACT MY PARTNER , MR. TRAP STILTON

Just then, it hit me. Trap was Smoothie's partner. That's why he wanted me to book a trip with Smoothie. He was making money off me. Oh, what a **CHEESEBRAIN** I'd been!

I ran to my cousin's thrift store, **CHEAP JUNK FOR LESS**.

There was a card in this window, too.

CLOSED, SUPER-CLOSED,
I'M AWAY, GOT IT?
I'M AT THE HIGH-CLASS
RODENT LUXURY RESORT.

LAUGHTER IS
CONTAGIOUS

I trudged to my office. I had to tell someone about my disastrous holiday. I poured out the whole story to my sister, Thea.

"Did you really swim with **sharks**? Did you really go **bungee jumping**? Did you really bike **twenty miles** to the hotel?" she snickered. Then she burst out laughing.

I was a bit hurt by her reaction. I had been looking for a shoulder to cry on. But Thea's shoulders were shaking with laughter. Tears streamed down her fur. "I haven't laughed this hard in years!" she shrieked. "Tell me again about the flashy swimsuit you bought. And were you really pestered by a mouselet named Bratfur?"

Now, as every rodent knows, **laughter is contagious**. Before I knew it, I was chuckling, too.

I mean, when I really thought about it, my adventures were **PRETTY FUNNY**.

The rest of my staff came in to see what all the noise was about. Soon my secretary, Mousella MacMouser; my editor in chief, Kreamy O'Cheddar; my art director, Merenguita Gingermouse; and my designers, Blasco Tabasco, Larry Keys, and Matt Wolf, were howling away with us. Even the cleaning mouse and the Xpress Delivery mouse joined in. Our laughter could be heard outside on the street. It infected many curious passers-by. Everyone wanted to hear the details of my incredibly **AWFUL, UNBELIEVABLE, ROTTEN, STINKING NIGHTMARE** holiday.

Right then, my sales manager, Shif T. Paws, entered the room. Do you know him? He's a rodent with a nose for business. One look at the hysterical crowd and I could see Shif's eyes light up.

He immediately pulled me aside. "Stilton, start writing a book about your adventure **RIGHT AWAY**!" he ordered. "We're going to sell **THOUSANDS, NO MILLIONS, NO BILLIONS** of copies. We'll be laughing all the way to the bank, I tell you!"

I scratched my whiskers. Writing a book is a lot of work. I wanted to think about it first. But as usual, Shif wouldn't take no for an answer. He began spouting dates and schedules. "Let's see, we'll bring it out for the CHRISTMAS season. That means I'll need your manuscript by next week, or maybe tomorrow, or maybe today."

He jumped up, clapping his paws. "Well, what are you waiting for, Stilton? Get moving, moving, **MOVING**!!!" he squeaked.

The others all agreed. I tried to argue, but Shif locked me in my office. I was stuck typing away at my computer **all day and all night**!

Are you curious about how it all ended? I finished the book in a jiffy. Two months later, it was turned into a movie script. When the movie was released, it broke all box office records. Yes, I am happy to squeak, **it was a fabumouse success!**

ABOUT THE AUTHOR

Born in New Mouse City, Mouse Island, GERONIMO STILTON is Rattus Emeritus of Mousomorphic Literature and of Neo-Ratonic Comparative Philosophy. For the past twenty years, he has been running The Rodent's Gazette, New Mouse City's most widely read daily newspaper.

Stilton was awarded the Ratitzer Prize for his scoops on *The Curse of the Cheese Pyramid* and *The Search for Sunken Treasure*. He has also received the Andersen Prize

for Personality of the Year. His works have been published all over the globe.

In his spare time, Mr. Stilton collects antique cheese rinds and plays golf. But what he most enjoys is telling stories to his nephew Benjamin.

THE RODENT'S GAZETTE

1. Main entrance
2. Printing presses (where everything is printed)
3. Accounts department
4. Editorial room (where editors, illustrators, and designers work)
5. Geronimo Stilton's office
6. Geronimo's botanical garden

MAP OF NEW MOUSE CITY

1. Industrial Zone
2. Cheese Factories
3. Angorat International Airport
4. WRAT Radio and Television Station
5. Cheese Market
6. Fish Market
7. Town Hall
8. Snotnose Castle
9. The Seven Hills of Mouse Island
10. Mouse Central Station
11. Trade Centre
12. Movie Theatre
13. Gym
14. Catnegie Hall
15. Singing Stone Plaza
16. The Gouda Theatre
17. Grand Hotel
18. Mouse General Hospital
19. Botanical Gardens
20. Cheap Junk for Less (Trap's store)
21. Parking Lot
22. Mouseum of Modern Art
23. University and Library
24. The Daily Rat
25. The Rodent's Gazette
26. Trap's House
27. Fashion District
28. The Mouse House Restaurant
29. Environmental Protection Centre
30. Harbour Office
31. Mousidon Square Garden
32. Golf Course
33. Swimming Pool
34. Blushing Meadow Tennis Courts
35. Curlyfur Island Amusement Park
36. Geronimo's House
37. Historic District
38. Public Library
39. Shipyard
40. Thea's House
41. New Mouse Harbour
42. Luna Lighthouse
43. The Statue of Liberty
44. Hercule Poirat's Office
45. Petunia Pretty Paws's House
46. Grandfather William's House

MAP OF MOUSE ISLAND

1. Big Ice Lake
2. Frozen Fur Peak
3. Slipperyslopes Glacier
4. Coldcreeps Peak
5. Ratzikistan
6. Transratania
7. Mount Vamp
8. Roastedrat Volcano
9. Brimstone Lake
10. Poopedcat Pass
11. Stinko Peak
12. Dark Forest
13. Vain Vampires Valley
14. Goosebumps Gorge
15. The Shadow Line Pass
16. Penny-Pincher Castle
17. Nature Reserve Park
18. Las Ratayas Marinas
19. Fossil Forest
20. Lake Lake
21. Lake Lakelake
22. Lake Lakelakelake
23. Cheddar Crag
24. Cannycat Castle
25. Valley of the Giant Sequoia
26. Cheddar Springs
27. Sulphurous Swamp
28. Old Reliable Geyser
29. Vole Vale
30. Ravingrat Ravine
31. Gnat Marshes
32. Munster Highlands
33. Mousehara Desert
34. Oasis of the Sweaty Camel
35. Cabbagehead Hill
36. Rattytrap Jungle
37. Rio Mosquito
38. Mousefort Beach
39. San Mouscisco
40. Swissville
41. Cheddarton
42. Mouseport
43. New Mouse City
44. Pirate Ship of Cats

HAVE YOU READ ALL OF GERONIMO'S ADVENTURES?

- *Lost Treasure of the Emerald Eye*
- *The Curse of the Cheese Pyramid*
- *Cat and Mouse in a Haunted House*
- *I'm Too Fond of My Fur!*
- *Four Mice Deep in the Jungle*
- *Paws Off, Cheddarface!*
- *Fangs and Feasts in Transratania*
- *Attack of the Pirate Cats*

☐ *A Fabumouse Holiday for Geronimo*

☐ *Hang on to Your Whiskers*

☐ *School Trip to Niagara Falls*

☐ *The Christmas Toy Factory*

☐ *Geronimo Stilton, Secret Agent*

☐ *A Fantastic School Adventure*

☐ *The Cheese Experiment*

☐ *The Super Chef Contest*

☐ *Welcome to Mouldy Manor*

☐ *The Treasure of Easter Island*

☐ *Mouse Overboard!*

☐ *This Hotel Is Haunted*

☐ *A Cheese-Coloured Camper Van*

- [ ] *The Search for Sunken Treasure*
- [ ] *The Ghost of the Underground*
- [ ] *The Mona Mousa Code*
- [ ] *Surf's Up, Geronimo!*
- [ ] *The Mystery of the Roaring Rat*
- [ ] *Merry Christmas, Geronimo!*
- [ ] *Shipwreck on Pirate Island*
- [ ] *The Temple of the Fire Ruby*
- [ ] *The Mouse Island Marathon*

HAPPY READING!